CHINESE FAIRY TALE

Little Colt Crosses the River

Adapted by Ming Yang

Illustrated by Chen Yongzhen

FOREIGN LANGUAGES PRESS   BEIJING

First Edition   1976
Second Edition   1986

The book was previously published under
the title of *A Foal Crosses the Stream*.

Hard Cover: ISBN 0-8351-1584-4
Paperback: ISBN 0-8351-1585-2

Copyright 1986 by Foreign Languages Press

Published by Foreign Languages Press
24 Baiwanzhuang Road, Beijing, China

Distributed by China International Book Trading Corporation
(Guoji Shudian), P.O. Box 399, Beijing, China

Printed in the People's Republic of China

In the countryside in China there are many horses — black ones, white ones, chestnut-coloured ... all colours.

Horses can pull carts, carry grain, fertilizer, firewood and straw. Sometimes people use horse carts to go to town and visit relatives.

Horses can also plough fields. Especially in busy spring and autumn they are the farmers' best helpers.

Oh! Look at this white colt, just as pretty as a picture! How his mother loves him!

One day the colt's mother asks him to take a sack of wheat to the miller. With the sack on his back he runs as fast as his legs can carry him.

On and on Little Colt runs until suddenly he comes to a gurgling river.

What to do? Little Colt runs to ask Old Ox. "Uncle Ox, is this river deep?" Old Ox replies, "The river is shallow. The water comes only up to my knees. I crossed the river just yesterday."

Little Colt is just about to cross the river when Little Squirrel runs up, shouting, "Don't cross, Little Colt! The water is very deep. My companion drowned yesterday when he tried to cross."

Old Ox says the water is shallow; Little Squirrel says the water is deep. Who's right? Little Colt can't decide, so he runs back to ask Mama.

"Why have you come back?" Mama Horse asks. Little Colt, embarrassed, replies, "I came to a river. Uncle Ox said the water was shallow, but Little Squirrel told me it was too deep to cross."

Mama Horse says, "The water is deep or it's shallow; you can or cannot cross. Have you thought it over carefully?" Little Colt, very embarrassed, shakes his head.

Mama Horse says kindly, "Uncle Ox is big and tall. Of course the river is shallow to him. Little Squirrel is small. Of course the river is deep. They both judged it by their own sizes. How about you? How do you compare with them?" Little Colt understands at once. He turns around and runs off.

Little Colt reaches the riverbank. Uncle Ox and Little Squirrel are still arguing. Neither will give in to the other.

Little Colt measures himself against the big, tall ox; he measures himself against the small squirrel. Then he says, "Let me try!"

Only after Little Colt jumps into the river does he know the water is not so shallow as Old Ox said and not so deep as Little Squirrel said. It comes just a little above his knees.

Little Colt easily crosses the river.

He delivers the wheat and returns home. Mama Horse praises him for doing so well.

Ever since, whenever Little Colt comes across something new, he first asks others about it, then he thinks it over before trying. That way, he is getting more and more competent.